Welcome to the World!

WAVE GOODBYE

BY **Rob Reid**

ILLUSTRATED BY **Lorraine Williams**   *October 1996*

LEE & LOW BOOKS Inc. • NEW YORK

Printed in Hong Kong by South China Printing Co. (1988) Ltd.

Book Design by Christy Hale
Book Production by Our House

The text is set in Italia.
The illustrations are rendered in watercolor, pastel, watercolor pencil, and gouache.

10 9 8 7 6 5 4 3 2 1
FIRST EDITION

Library of Congress Cataloging-in-Publication Data
Reid, Rob
Wave goodbye/by Rob Reid; illustrated by Lorraine Williams. — 1st ed.
p.   cm.
Summary: Characters perform motor activities and exercise the entire body
as they celebrate all the ways to wave goodbye by using elbows, lips, hair, and finally hands.
ISBN 1-880000-30-X (hardcover)
[1. Motor learning—Fiction. 2. Exercise—Fiction. 3. Stories in rhyme.] I. Williams, Lorraine, ill. II. Title.
PZ8.3.R267Wav 1996   95-21733
[E]—dc20   CIP AC

To Helen Mary Goff Reid—R.R.

For Pete, an unmatched pal and confederate—L.W.

Wave high,

wave low,

I think it's time,

we gotta go.

Wave your elbows,

wave your toes.

Wave your tongue,

and wave your nose.

Wave your knees,

wave your lips.

Blow a kiss

with fingertips.

Wave your ears,

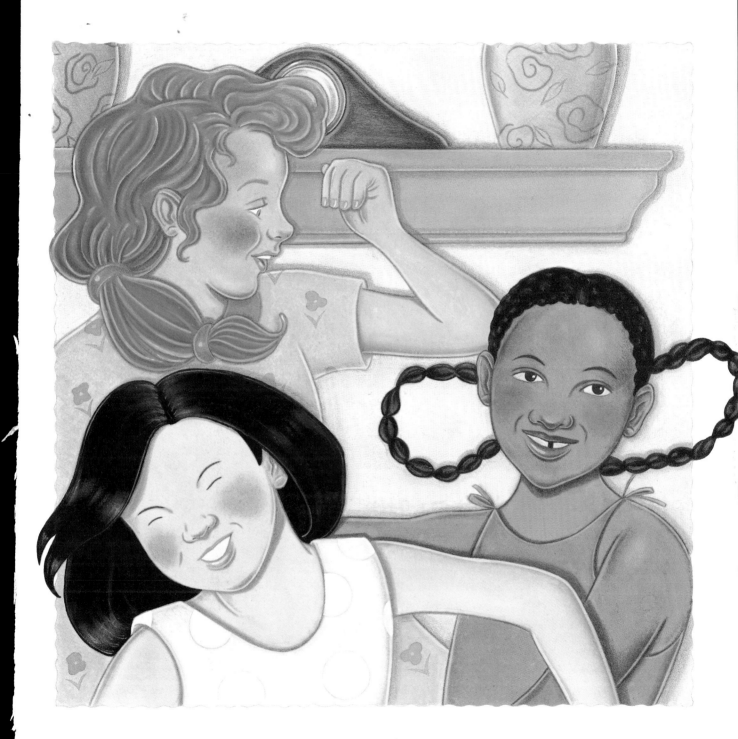

wave your hair.

Wave your belly

and derriere.

Wave your chin,

wave your eye.

Wave your hand and say goodbye!